Carolyn Newcomer
2010

The Adventures of a Sick Bag Book Series

Barf's

First Flight

Lessons In Helping Others

The Adventures of a Sick Bag Book Series

Barf's
First Flight

Lessons In Helping Others

Written by Carolyn Newcomer

Illustrated by C. Andrea Raschke

WHITE STAG PRESS
A DIVISION OF
PUBLISHERS DESIGN GROUP, INC.
ROSEVILLE, CALIFORNIA 95678

ISBN 13: 978-0979258381
Library of Congress Control: 2008910370

WHITE STAG PRESS
a division of
Publishers Design Group, Inc.
Roseville, California 95678
www.publishersdesign.com
1.800.587.6666

Printed in China

For my three children

Max, Ashley, and Hunter.

I love you more than you know.

Acknowledgments

Max, I will forever hold dear in my heart that inspiring flight to Palm Springs—without you, there would be no Barf. To my sweet Ashley, your delicate constitution has provided a never ending source of story lines. And to Hunter, with your vivid imagination, may we always travel together on big adventures. I would like to thank and acknowledge the unending support of my husband—"Go for it, dear!" was his mantra. Thank you to Lisa Doig and Kerry Wells for taking time from their busy lives to help with the initial editing and proofreading. And to Robert Brekke of Publishers Design Group, Inc., believing we had a solid concept on which to work and build.

Barf was created to inspire the love of adventure and travel in children, while teaching a lesson in kindness and compassion to those in need.

As a parent, I wanted to educate my three children on the importance of helping those less fortunate. *How can I help?*, is the question I wanted them to ask of themselves. But where do parents start? They start by simply teaching their children, by example, to be kind to others every day with a willingness to lend a helping hand. This belief system is at the core of Barf's spirit.

No one loves adventure more than Barf and Tiny. They are willing to go anywhere and do anything just to help anyone in their time of need. Interlaced with irreverent humor and a message of kindness, the book series, *The Adventures of a Sick Bag,* will take your child around the world and beyond!

Barf was excited. Today would be his first day of adventure in helping those in need. He was very proud of his duties. He had come from a long line of bag descendents. His father, Boot, was a bag. His mother's mother, Grandma Bucket, and his great Uncle Chunk, were bags.

Filled with anticipation, Barf thought to himself, "Will I travel the high seas? Will I be needed at an amusement park? Or, maybe I'll be sent to a hospital!"

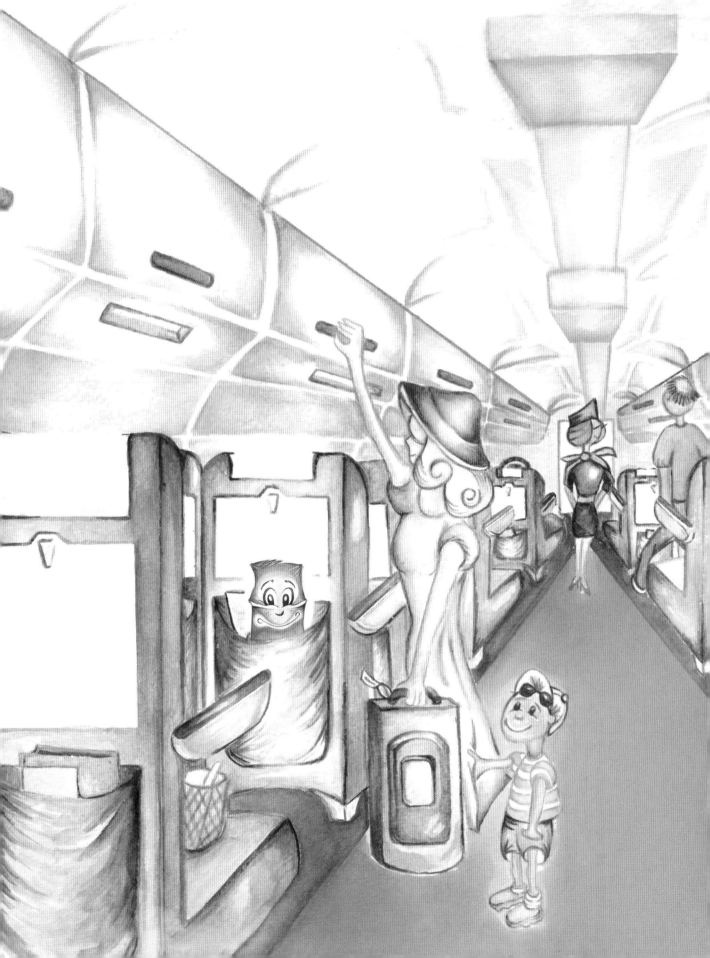

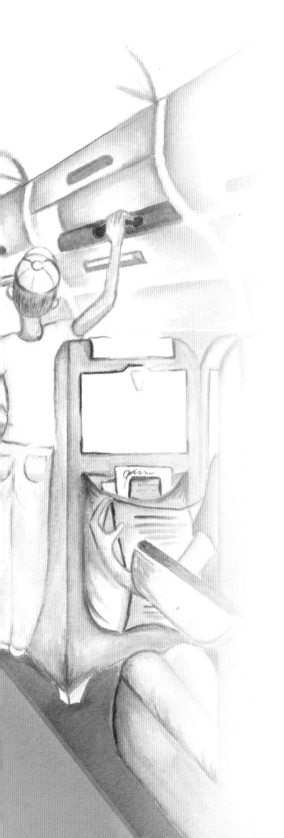

Barf's first assignment was to find himself behind the seat in a big airplane. Nestled in the pocket in the back of the chair, Barf Boy, the sick bag, waited for the airplane to take off. He watched anxiously as the line of people searched for their correct seats.

"Look!" Barf smiled to himself. "A young boy and his mother are heading my way!" Barf peeked over to watch as the boy and his mother stowed their belongings in the overhead compartment.

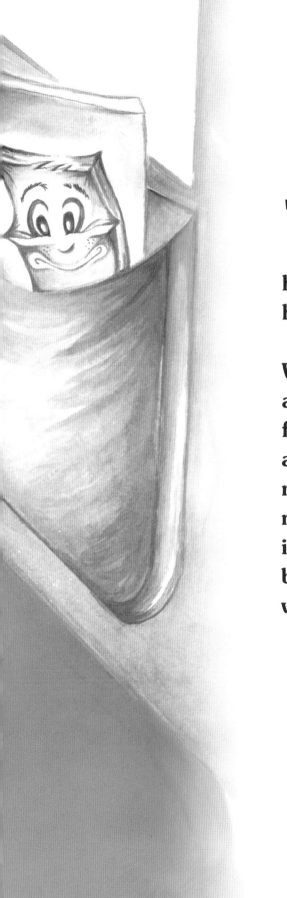

arf thought, "They must be going somewhere special. The little boy is wearing a hat and sun glasses. And his mom has a big beach bag."

With a roar of the engines, the airplane moved. Barf knew from family stories, that while riding aboard an airplane, he could be needed at any moment! He wanted more than anything to be there in time of need, should someone begin to feel sick. Barf began to wonder, "Will I be needed soon?"

Most of the passengers seemed to be enjoying the flight. Some people read books, some played cards, and others just listened to music. The small boy seemed to be happy coloring in his coloring book and playing games with his mom.

It had been a smooth flight so far and he was about to give up hope, when all of a sudden, the plane began to jump and jumble up and down.

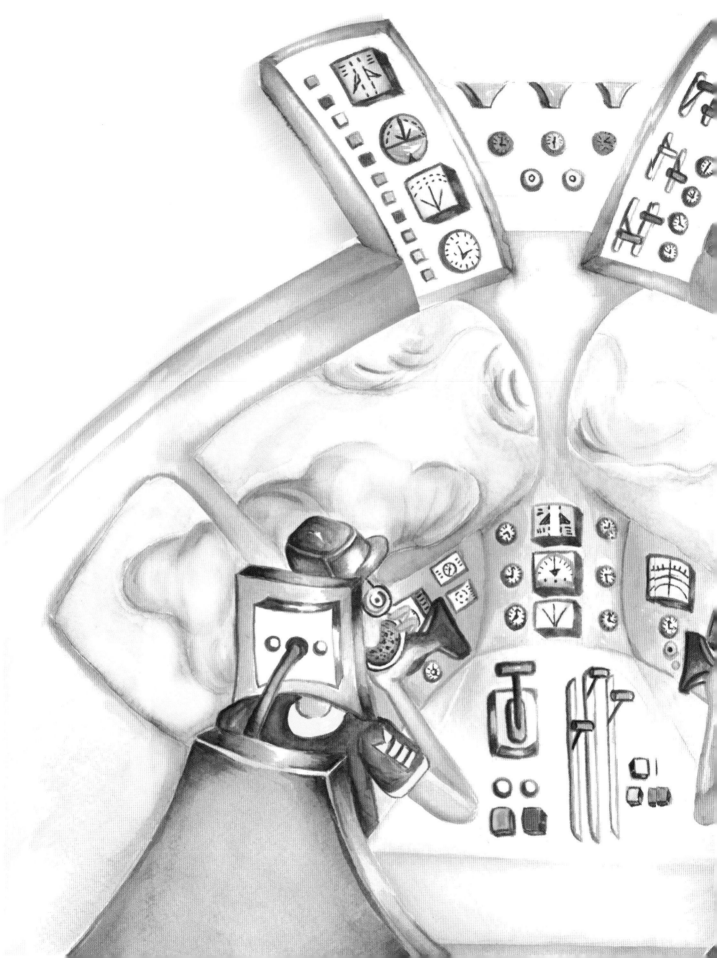

L adies and gentlemen," announced the pilot over the intercom, "please fasten your seat belts. Due to the thunderstorm we are passing through, this is going to be a bumpy ride as we approach our landing."

Like the downhill motion of a roller coaster, the plane dropped! The rocking and tossing of the plane caused many of the passengers to feel ill and reach for their sick bags. But the little boy and his mother were laughing and raising their arms.

"Wheee! Woo Hoo," they cried!

"Mommy, this is just like the Hooty Hurl Roller Coaster at the beach!"

Unbelievable! Barf's first chance to help someone in need, and instead, the boy and his mother were laughing with delight.

Just then, Barf noticed a young woman frantically searching the seat pocket for a bag. She gasped, bit her lips and turned two shades of polar white. Barf could tell by her expression that she was in desperate need of a bag, but she could not find one.

Barf, with all his might, wriggled from his seat pocket to reach the airsick passenger.

Suddenly the plane lurched to the left and Barf went flying out of his seat pocket and slid down and under all the seats. Barf was dizzy and dazed. With stars in his eyes, he wondered how he was going to help. He knew he needed to get to her quickly.

"Excuse me folks, this is your pilot speaking. It seems that we will need to circle the airport one more time."

The plane shifted and Barf slid under the seats and stopped at the feet of the young woman. But it was too late; the woman had found her own bag.

Barf watched as she wiped the sweat from her brow. She must be feeling more like herself again," thought Barf. "I can see the color of her cheeks return, they are not so pale anymore."

Although Barf was glad the woman was feeling better, his heart was broken. It turned out that Barf's best friend, Hurl, from the sick-bag factory, was there to help the woman instead.

Tears began to fall down Barf's cheeks, when out of the corner of his eye he noticed a small, discouraged tissue.

"What's wrong little tissue?"

The tissue sniffled and said, "I wasn't there to help the sick passenger. My family is going to be so disappointed when they hear this. Maybe if I had popped out of my tissue box a little quicker, she would have noticed me."

"And if I hadn't slid head first under the seats, she would have noticed me too," said Barf.

"**H**ey," piped the tissue, "since neither of us could be there for her, maybe we could work together the next time."

"Great idea!" responded Barf. "What is your name little tissue?"

"My family back at home in our box calls me Tiny."

"My name is Barf Boy, but you can call me Barf."

While the two friends were getting to know each other, Tiny heard a familiar sound coming from the young boy.

aah....aaah....chooo!" Barf and Tiny looked at each other with excitement! This could be Tiny's moment!

Determined to help, Tiny ran to the boy's side.

It was too late, the boy sneezed with all his might into a hand-embroidered handkerchief. It was the kind of handkerchief Tiny had heard about, decorated with scalloped edging and pretty flowers in the corners.

The fancy handkerchief looked into Tiny's sad eyes with a snobbish glare, "Better luck next time, toilet paper square! Let's face it, you're just not made of the right stuff. I am genuine French linen, made especially for a job like this. I am soft, pretty, and can be used over and over again."

Fighting back the tears, Tiny slumped to his knees in shame.

Barf scurried to Tiny's side, understanding his friend's hurt and embarrassment.

"Don't listen to that uppity piece of linen. Just because she can be washed and reused again doesn't make her better than you, Tiny."

"But she's right Barf, I'm just a little square of tissue, I can be used for toilet paper, the lowest of the low."

"Tiny, you have a caring, giving heart. You are willing to sacrifice yourself to help people in need."

Thanks," sniffled Tiny. "But I don't feel like we did anything to help."

"Well, I think we helped each other," said Barf. "We encouraged each other when we were both feeling down." Tiny smiled.

At last the airplane went bump, bump and the friends bounced across the aisle into the little boy's beach bag.

T he plane stopped. Barf and Tiny felt themselves being hoisted onto the shoulder of the little boy's mother.

"Thank you for flying with Sunshine Airlines," said the flight attendant.

Barf and Tiny had been there for each other in their time of need, when both were feeling sad. They learned their first important lesson in friendship; sometimes opportunities to help others can come in unexpected ways.

Together, their friendship will continue to grow as they travel on new adventures around the world and beyond.

The Adventures of a Sick Bag Book Series

Carolyn Newcomer continues to write and create new adventures for Barf and his friends.

Barf's First Flight: Lessons In Helping Others, is the first of an ongoing series with Barf helping those in need as he travels the world and beyond. Barf and Tiny learn their first lesson in true friendship.

Other Barf stories include:
Barf on the Beach: Barf and Tiny meet kind-hearted Peppy Dot. When they encounter rough seas on a tropical snorkeling vacation, the threesome discover the power of teamwork.

Barf Goes Up: Barf and Tiny accidentally stumble into the launch of a space shuttle where everything goes up! The inseparable pair learn a valuable lesson in following rules in order to stay safe.

Barf in the Hospital: Barf and Tiny reach out to the truly needy when they stop in for a visit to a children's hospital. This is a story of hope and inspiration with Cousin Spew coming to the rescue!

Barf Winds Down: There is trouble ahead on a narrow and curvy road as Barf and Tiny go on a drive through the hills of Mexico. Traveling together, they learn to connect with a different culture and lifestyle.

For online ordering of books: www.barfsbooks.com

Published to the book trade by
White Stag Press
a division of
Publishers Design Group, Inc.
www.publishersdesign.com